☆ THE ADVENTURES OF ☆
TINTIN

THE ADVENTURES OF TINTIN: TINTIN'S DARING ESCAPE
A BANTAM BOOK 978 0 857 51078 5

First published in the United States in 2011 by Little Brown

First published in Great Britain by Bantam,
an imprint of Random House Children's Books
A Random House Group Company

Bantam edition published 2011

1 3 5 7 9 10 8 6 4 2

Bantam Books are published by Random House Children's Books,
61–63 Uxbridge Road, London W5 5SA

www.**kids**at**randomhouse**.co.uk
www.**totallyrandombooks**.co.uk
www.**randomhouse**.co.uk

Addresses for companies within The Random House Group Limited can be found at: www.randomhouse.co.uk/offices.htm

THE RANDOM HOUSE GROUP Limited Reg. No. 954009

A CIP catalogue record for this book is available from the British Library.

Printed in Great Britain by Print 4 Limited.

★ THE ADVENTURES OF ★
TINTIN

TINTIN'S DARING ESCAPE

Adapted by Kirsten Mayer

Screenplay by Steven Moffat and Edgar Wright & Joe Cornish

Based on The Adventures of Tintin series by Hergé

BANTAM BOOKS

Tintin walks with his faithful terrier, Snowy, puzzling over a new mystery. They recently discovered a secret message inside a model of a ship named the *Unicorn*.

They found a small scroll with a poem on it inside the ship's mast. The real *Unicorn* was a very old ship that patrolled the seas in search of pirates. Sir Francis Haddock was the captain when the ship, filled with treasure, sank to the bottom of the ocean.

"This is our lead, Snowy, I wonder what it means."

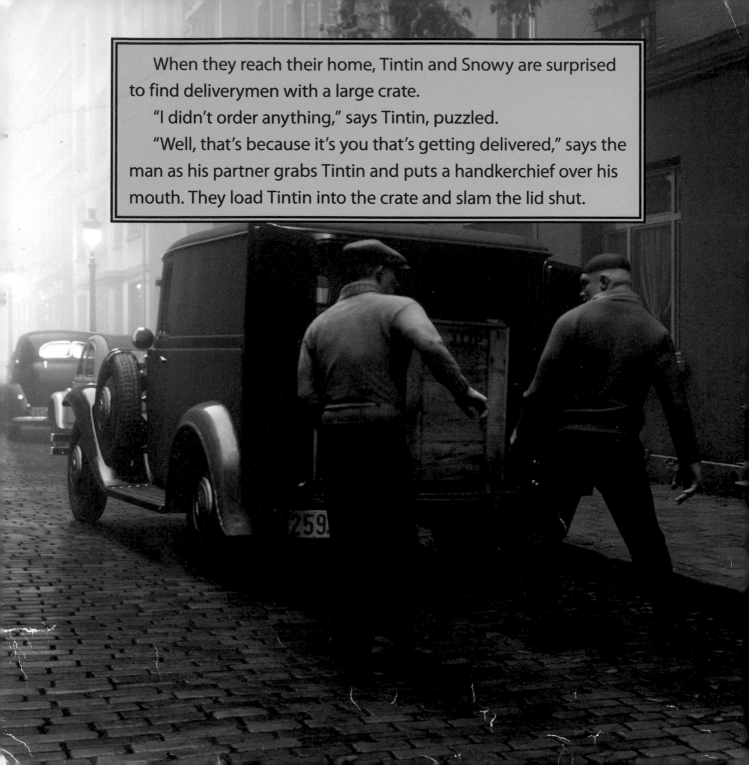

When they reach their home, Tintin and Snowy are surprised to find deliverymen with a large crate.

"I didn't order anything," says Tintin, puzzled.

"Well, that's because it's you that's getting delivered," says the man as his partner grabs Tintin and puts a handkerchief over his mouth. They load Tintin into the crate and slam the lid shut.

Snowy bites one of the men on his leg, but the thug shakes him off. Snowy watches them load Tintin's crate into the van and drive off down the street. Snowy follows the van all the way to the docks, where he sees Tintin's crate get loaded onto a giant ship.

Snowy sneaks aboard by scampering across the ropes.

Tintin wakes up on board the ship, tied up in a room with just one porthole. The two "deliverymen" are there with a third man – their boss.

"Where is it?" the third man asks Tintin. "The second scroll from your ship."

"I don't have it," replies Tintin, knowing the man must mean the secret paper he found in his model ship. "You said the second one. So there is more than one?"

"I will find it, with or without your help. Think about exactly how useful you are to me," the boss threatens.

The men leave and lock the door behind them – but not before a white blur shoots into the room. It's Snowy!

"Snowy!" cries Tintin. "It's good to see you! Can you chew through these ropes?"

After Snowy frees him, Tintin takes a look around his prison. The door is locked. He looks out the porthole but sees only the wide-open ocean rushing past. He looks up and sees another porthole. Tintin gets an idea.

He grabs some loose boards in a corner of the room and ties them together with his rope. Then he tosses them up to the other porthole. The boards sail through the other opening and when he pulls on the rope, the boards catch on the sides of the window and hold tight.

"Come on, Snowy! Let's go!" Tintin and Snowy crawl out through the porthole and climb up the rope. They push themselves in through the other porthole and land on the floor.

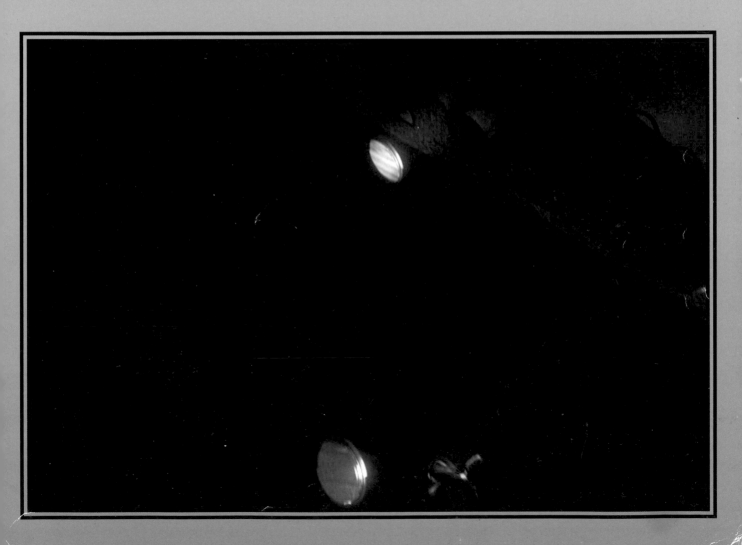

The room is not empty. An older man springs to his feet when he sees Snowy. "The giant rat of Sumatra!" he cries. Then he sees Tintin, and he grabs a broken chair leg for a weapon. "Thought you could sneak in here and catch me with my trousers down, eh?"

Tintin snatches up another chair leg. "I'd rather you kept your trousers on, if it's all the same to you."

"You're one of them!" the man cries, jabbing at Tintin with the chair leg.

"You've got it all wrong," says Tintin. "I was kidnapped!"

"The filthy swine!" the man shouts. "That man turned my whole crew against me. He took my ship!"

"You're the captain?" asks Tintin.

"Of course I'm the captain," the man scoffs. "I've been locked in this room for days."

Tintin tries the door, and it opens easily. It's not locked!

"Oh, well," stammers the captain, embarrassed, "I *assumed* it was locked."

"Excuse me," says Tintin. "I have to keep moving so I can get off this tub."

As Tintin steps into the hallway the captain follows him.
"I'm Tintin, by the way," says Tintin. "This is Snowy."
"Haddock. Archibald Haddock," the captain says. "There's a lifeboat up on the deck we can get away in. Follow me."

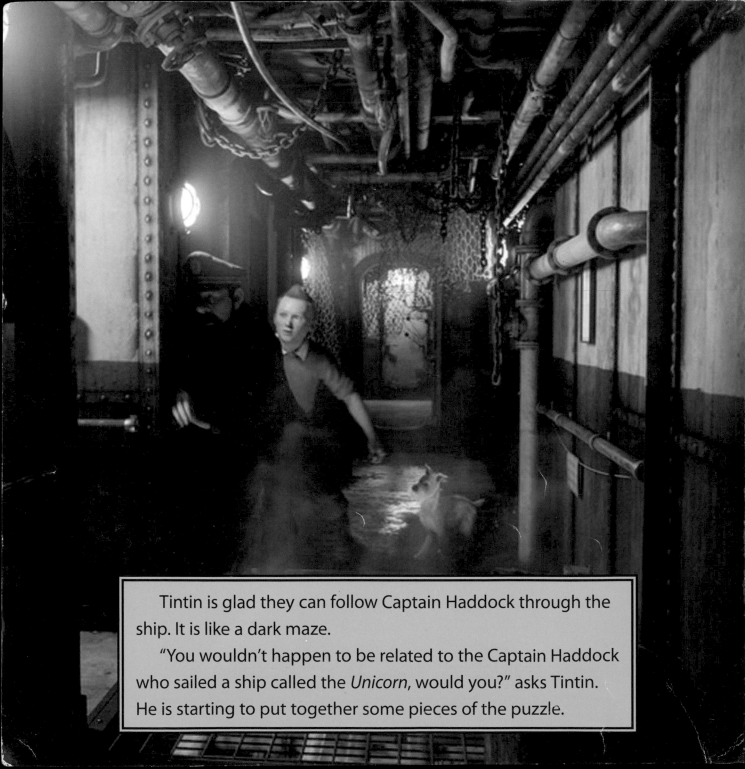

Tintin is glad they can follow Captain Haddock through the ship. It is like a dark maze.

"You wouldn't happen to be related to the Captain Haddock who sailed a ship called the *Unicorn*, would you?" asks Tintin. He is starting to put together some pieces of the puzzle.

"What do you know of the *Unicorn*?" asks the captain. "The secret of that ship is known only to my family. It has been passed down...but I've forgotten it."

"Is there somebody else in the family who would know?" asks Tintin.

"No, the *Unicorn* captain had three sons, but I am the last of the Haddocks."

"Three sons!" cries Tintin. "That's what the scroll said! Three ships for three sons! There must be a third model ship, and that is what this guy is looking for!"

"What are you raving on about?" Haddock asks.

They go through the door and race out onto the dark deck. "Hurry up, Captain! We've no time to lose!"

They start to push one of the lifeboats toward the edge of the ship. Tintin hears a noise, and they quickly hide as some of the thugs move out through one door and in another.

"What's that?" asks Tintin.

"The radio room," replies Haddock.

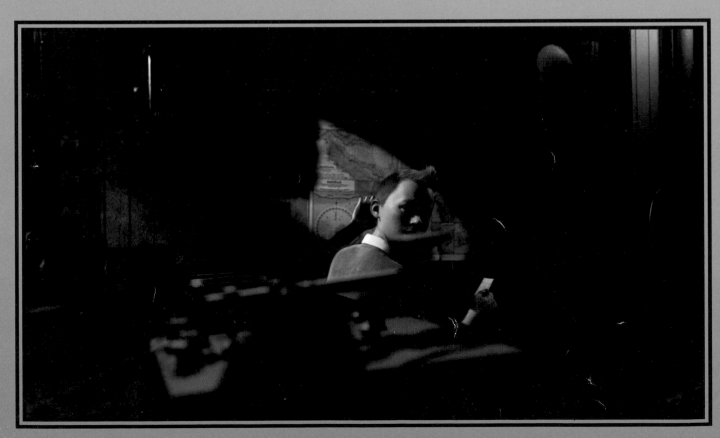

Tintin sneaks over to the radio room door and overhears a Morse code message coming over the wireless radio. He and Snowy sneak into the room. Snowy finds a sandwich. Tintin finds a map and a brochure about the city of Bagghar.

"The sultanate of Bagghar on the Red Sea," Tintin reads aloud. "Let's go, Snowy. We have our next clue!"

Outside, Haddock is about to drop the boat into the water. But he is surprised to find a sailor sleeping inside!

"Hey!" the sailor shouts. "Put your hands up!"

Haddock raises his hands, dropping the rope that was holding the boat. The lifeboat and sailor both splash into the water below. "Let that be a lesson to you!" cries the captain.

He unties the next lifeboat as Tintin and Snowy race across the deck. Snowy jumps in first, and Haddock follows, letting one rope loose. The boat dangles by one rope as the crew starts firing on them! Tintin hops in just as the enemy fire slices through the rope and they drop into the sea.

"Stay low!" says Tintin as they row away.

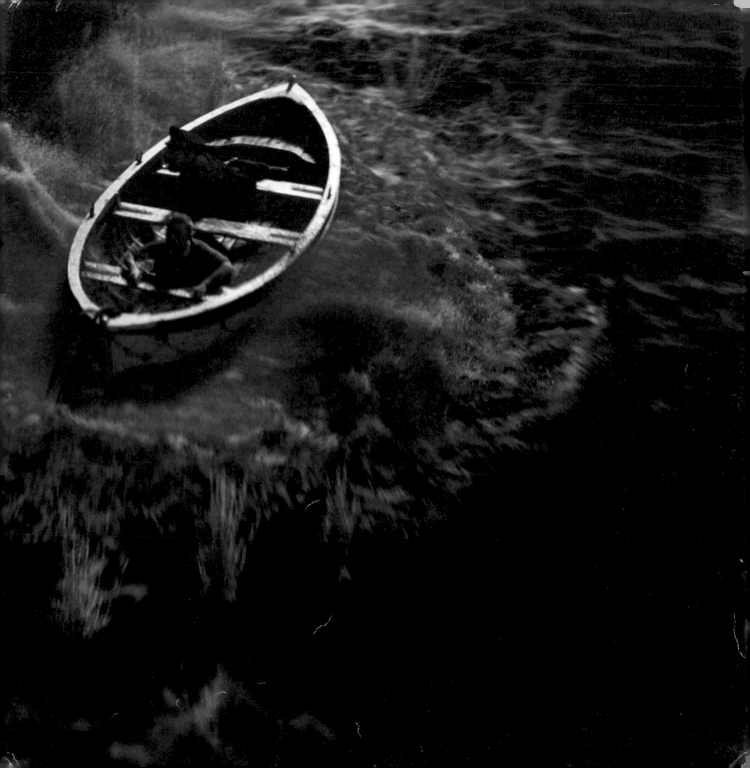

Soon, they are far enough away to feel safe.

"We have to get to Bagghar to find the third *Unicorn*," Tintin tells the captain. "I know that only a true Haddock can discover the secret of the *Unicorn*. How's your thirst for adventure, Captain?"

"Unquenchable!" cries Haddock.